Robin Hoods

Mary Elizabeth Salzmann
Illustrated by Anne Haberstroh

Consulting Editor, Diane Craig, M.A./Reading Specialist

Published by ABDO Publishing Company, 4940 Viking Drive, Edina, Minnesota 55435.

Printed in the United States.

Credits
Edited by: Pam Price
Curriculum Coordinator: Nancy Tuminelly
Cover and Interior Design and Production: Mighty Media
Photo Credits: Cal Vornberger/Peter Arnold Inc., Corbis Images, Corel, ShutterStock

Library of Congress Cataloging-in-Publication Data

Salzmann, Mary Elizabeth, 1980-
     Robin hoods / Mary Elizabeth Salzmann; illustrated by Anne Haberstroh.
        p. cm. -- (Fact & fiction. Critter chronicles)
     Summary: Rusty and Ruby, two robins, work hard to put together outfits for a costume party. Alternating pages provide facts about robins.
     ISBN 10 1-59928-466-9 (hardcover)
     ISBN 10 1-59928-467-7 (paperback)

     ISBN 13 978-1-59928-466-8 (hardcover)
     ISBN 13 978-1-59928-467-5 (paperback)
     [1. Costume--Fiction. 2. Parties--Fiction. 3. Robins--Fiction.] I. Haberstroh, Anne, ill. II. Title. III. Series.
     PZ7.S15565Rob 2007
     [E]--dc22
                                                                                              2006005702

SandCastle Level: Fluent

SandCastle™ books are created by a professional team of educators, reading specialists, and content developers around five essential components—phonemic awareness, phonics, vocabulary, text comprehension, and fluency—to assist young readers as they develop reading skills and strategies and increase their general knowledge. All books are written, reviewed, and leveled for guided reading, early reading intervention, and Accelerated Reader® programs for use in shared, guided, and independent reading and writing activities to support a balanced approach to literacy instruction. The SandCastle™ series has four levels that correspond to early literacy development. The levels help teachers and parents select appropriate books for young readers.

Emerging Readers	**Beginning Readers**	**Transitional Readers**	**Fluent Readers**
(no flags)	(1 flag)	(2 flags)	(3 flags)

These levels are meant only as a guide. All levels are subject to change.

FACT & FiCTiON

This series provides early fluent readers the opportunity to develop reading comprehension strategies and increase fluency. These books are appropriate for guided, shared, and independent reading.

FACT The left-hand pages incorporate realistic photographs to enhance readers' understanding of informational text.

FiCTiON The right-hand pages engage readers with an entertaining, narrative story that is supported by whimsical illustrations.

The Fact and Fiction pages can be read separately to improve comprehension through questioning, predicting, making inferences, and summarizing. They can also be read side-by-side, in spreads, which encourages students to explore and examine different writing styles.

FACT OR **FiCTiON?** This fun quiz helps reinforce students' understanding of what is real and not real.

SPEED READ The text-only version of each section includes word-count rulers for fluency practice and assessment.

GLOSSARY Higher-level vocabulary and concepts are defined in the glossary.

SandCastle™ would like to hear from you.

Tell us your stories about reading this book. What was your favorite page? Was there something hard that you needed help with? Share the ups and downs of learning to read. To get posted on the ABDO Publishing Company Web site, send us an e-mail at:

sandcastle@abdopublishing.com

3

American robins measure 8 to 11 inches from head to tail. Male and female robins look similar, except males have brighter colors.

Rusty and Ruby are very excited about the Robin's Roost Community Center costume party. Ruby says, "It's going to be a lot of fun, but I really wish Rosa were coming. She said she has something else she has to do that day."

RRCC

COSTUME PARTY

Robins live all across North America. They are found anywhere there are trees.

Rusty and Ruby work hard on their costumes. Rusty is going as Robin Hood. He makes a bow and arrows out of a small tree branch and some twigs. "Now I just need to ask Uncle Rufus if I can borrow his green hat," he says.

The female robin builds the nest using twigs, grass, and leaves held together with mud. She lines the nest with moss and soft grasses.

Ruby weaves a basket as part of her Little Red Riding Hood costume. "This basket and my red cape will make my costume perfect," she declares.

Robins are black and dark gray with distinctive red-orange chests.

When they get to the community center, Rusty shouts, "Wow! The decorations are really cool!"

"Absolutely," Ruby agrees. "Look! There's even a life-size statue of a robin!"

Robins eat worms, insects, and fruit. They find food primarily by sight rather than by smell or sound.

They see their friend
Reid, who is dressed as a
wizard. "Hello, Reid," Rusty and
Ruby chirp.

There are lots of fun activities and
games. First they bob for berries.

Robins lay three to five light-blue eggs at a time. The eggs take about two weeks to hatch.

Next they play pin the egg on the nest. Rusty's egg ends up under the nest. "Hey, Rusty," Reid teases, "Chicks need to hatch before they can fly!"

RUBY

RUSTY

Robins have a wingspan of 12 to 16 inches. Like other birds, robins' bones are hollow. This makes their bodies light, so flying is easier.

When it's time for the costume contest, everyone is confused when the judge awards first place to the robin statue. Suddenly the statue shouts, "Surprise!"

Ruby gasps, "Is that you, Rosa?"

"Yes!" Rosa says. "I'm a hood ornament!"

"I didn't even recognize you!" Ruby exclaims. "I'm so glad you came after all!"

17

In the winter, robins gather in large groups called roosts. There can be over 100,000 robins in a single roost.

"Me too!" Rosa says. "And now that the contest is over, I can move around and have some fun!"

Just then the music starts, and they all head for the dance floor. "This is the best Robin's Roost costume party ever!" Ruby proclaims.

19

FACT or Fiction?

Read each statement below. Then decide whether it's from the FACT section or the Fiction section!

1. Male and female robins look alike.

2. Robins make costumes to wear to parties.

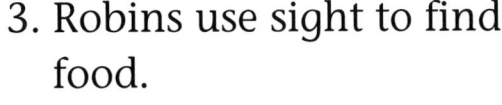

3. Robins use sight to find food.

4. Robins play pin the egg on the nest.

ANSWERS
1. fact 2. fiction 3. fact 4. fiction

American robins measure 8 to 11 inches from head   9
to tail. Male and female robins look similar, except   18
males have brighter colors.   22

Robins live all across North America. They are found   31
anywhere there are trees.   35

The female robin builds the nest using twigs, grass,   44
and leaves held together with mud. She lines the nest   54
with moss and soft grasses.   59

Robins are black and dark gray with distinctive red-   68
orange chests.   70

Robins eat worms, insects, and fruit. They find food   79
primarily by sight rather than by smell or sound.   88

Robins lay three to five light-blue eggs at a time.   99
The eggs take about two weeks to hatch.   107

Robins have a wingspan of 12 to 16 inches. Like   117
other birds, robins' bones are hollow. This makes their   126
bodies light, so flying is easier.   132

In the winter, robins gather in large groups called   141
roosts. There can be over 100,000 robins in a single roost.   152

Rusty and Ruby are very excited about the   8
Robin's Roost Community Center costume party.   14
Ruby says, "It's going to be a lot of fun, but I   26
really wish Rosa were coming. She said she has   35
something else she has to do that day."   43

Rusty and Ruby work hard on their costumes.   51
Rusty is going as Robin Hood. He makes a bow   61
and arrows out of a small tree branch and some   71
twigs. "Now I just need to ask Uncle Rufus if I   82
can borrow his green hat," he says.   89

Ruby weaves a basket as part of her Little Red   99
Riding Hood costume. "This basket and my red   107
cape will make my costume perfect," she declares.   115

When they get to the community center, Rusty   123
shouts, "Wow! The decorations are really cool!"   130

"Absolutely," Ruby agrees. "Look! There's even   136
a life-size statue of a robin!"   143

They see their friend Reid, who is dressed as a   153
wizard. "Hello, Reid," Rusty and Ruby chirp.   160

There are lots of fun activities and games. First they bob for berries.

Next they play pin the egg on the nest. Rusty's egg ends up under the nest. "Hey, Rusty," Reid teases, "Chicks need to hatch before they can fly!"

When it's time for the costume contest, everyone is confused when the judge awards first place to the robin statue. Suddenly the statue shouts, "Surprise!"

Ruby gasps, "Is that you, Rosa?"

"Yes!" Rosa says. "I'm a hood ornament!"

"I didn't even recognize you!" Ruby exclaims. "I'm so glad you came after all!"

"Me too!" Rosa says. "And now that the contest is over, I can move around and have some fun!"

Just then the music starts, and they all head for the dance floor. "This is the best Robin's Roost costume party ever!" Ruby proclaims.

GLOSSARY

decoration. an item that is displayed to make something or someplace look festive or pretty

distinctive. having a special feature that sets one apart from the others

hood ornament. a decoration attached to the front of a car or truck

moss. a short, fuzzy green plant that grows on soil as well as surfaces such as rocks and trees

North America. the continent that includes Canada, the United States, and Mexico, as well as other countries

wingspan. the distance from one wing tip to the other when the wings are fully spread

To see a complete list of SandCastle™ books and other nonfiction titles from ABDO Publishing Company, visit www.abdopublishing.com or contact us at: 4940 Viking Drive, Edina, Minnesota 55435 • 1-800-800-1312 • fax: 1-952-831-1632